Tips for Reading Together

Children learn best when reading is fun.

- Talk about the title and the pictures on the cover.
- Look through the pictures together so your child can see what the story is about.
- Read the story to your child, placing your finger under the words as you read.
- Have fun finding the hidden feather.
- Read the story again and encourage your child to join in.
- Give lots of praise as your child reads with you.

Children enjoy reading stories again and again.
This helps to build their confidence.

Have fun!

Find the feather hidden in every picture.

Mum's New Hat

Written by Roderick Hunt
Illustrated by Alex Brychta

OXFORD
UNIVERSITY PRESS

Mum had a new hat.

The wind blew.

It blew Mum's hat off.

"Get my hat," said Mum.

Dad ran.

The wind blew.

Oh no!

"Get that hat," said Dad.

Kipper ran.

The wind blew.

Oh no!

"Get that hat," said Kipper.

Biff ran.

The wind blew.

Oh no!

"Look at my new hat!"
said Mum.

Think about the story

How did Mum lose her new hat?

Why do you think Biff has a camera?

What funny things happened to Mum's hat?

What has happened to you on windy days?

A maze

Help Mum get her hat.

Useful common words repeated in this story and
other books at Level 1.

get   my   said   the
Names in this story: Mum   Dad   Biff   Kipper

More books for you to enjoy

Level 1: Getting Ready

Level 2: Starting to Read

Level 3: Becoming a Reader

Level 4: Building Confidence

Level 5: Reading with Confidence

OXFORD
UNIVERSITY PRESS

Great Clarendon Street,
Oxford OX2 6DP

Text © Roderick Hunt 2006
Illustrations © Alex Brychta 2006

First published 2006

Series Editors: Kate Ruttle,
Annemarie Young

British Library Cataloguing
in Publication Data available

ISBN–13: 978-019-279226-6

10 9 8 7 6 5 4 3

Printed in China by Imago

Have more fun with Read at Home